Waddle, Waddle, Quack, Quack, Quack

For my mother, Anna, the original writer and reader in the family who generously shared
her love of language and books—with deep gratitude and much love. —B. A. S.

To Matthew and Amira Jean Long.
As you start your new life together, be gentle with each other. "Strive to be happy." —S. L.

ISBN 0-439-81982-2

12 11 10 9 8 7 6 5 4 3 2 1   6 7 8 9 10 11/0

Printed in the U.S.A.   08

First Scholastic printing, March 2006

Book design by Sara Gillingham.

Typeset in Marc Anthony and Walbaum.

The illustrations in this book were rendered in pen and ink with watercolor.

Waddle, Waddle, Quack, Quack, Quack

by Barbara Anne Skalak ✦ illustrated by Sylvia Long

SCHOLASTIC INC.

New York   Toronto   London   Auckland   Sydney
Mexico City   New Delhi   Hong Kong   Buenos Aires

What's that pecking? *Tap, tap, tap!*
   Eggs start splitting. *Crack, crack, crack.*
Mama paces up and back.
   Waddle, waddle, *quack, quack, quack.*

Broken eggshells fall away.
Five new ducklings start their day.
Bobbling, wobbling, testing legs.
The world is big outside their eggs!

Small feet racing. Go, go, go!

Chasing Mama, don't be slow!

Hawks swoop low, then circle high.

Walk with Mama, stay close by.

To the lakeside, plop on in.
Copy Mama. Take a swim.

Heads down under, rear ends up.

Tasty pondweeds. *Glup, glup, glup.*

As the ducklings dip and feed,
        one drifts off between the reeds.
He looks for Mama—left then right—
        but Mama's disappeared from sight!

Blue sky darkens, lightning flashes.

Boom! Boom! Boom! Thunder crashes.

Big waves growing, going's tough.

Which way back? The lake's too rough!

Little duckling all alone
        must find Mama on his own.
Cross the meadow, wild and wide,
        flowers waving side to side.

Where is Mama?
In this grass?

Near these daisies?
On this path?

Around this rock?
Behind this tree?

Where else could Mama be?

Up this hill?

Just pinecones, needles.

In this log?

Big ants and beetles!

Down this hole?

Peek in to see—*whoops!*
Where else could Mama be?

On the lake still? Water's clearing.
  Breaks of sun, clouds disappearing.
Dash downhill—okay to swim!
  Little duckling—*splash*—dives in.

Through the shallows to the deep.
Calling Mama, *peep, peep, peep.*

"I'm here!" cries Mama. *Quack! Quack! Quack!*
"And here you are! You made it back!"

Ducklings know who Mama's found.
They paddle close and gather round.
"What did you see? What did you do?"
Peep, peep, peep! "We all missed you!"

Dusk is falling, screech owls hoot.
　　"Stay up front," says Mama. "Scoot!
No more roaming off alone.
　　Keep together, let's head home."

Safe inside their cozy nest,
    tired ducklings—time to rest.
Fluffy puffs of gold and brown,
    preening, dozing, nestled down.

A few last whispers, *peep, peep, peep,*
    as drowsy ducklings drift to sleep.
Moon climbs in her bed of black.
    "Sweet dreams," says Mama. *Quack, quack, quack.*